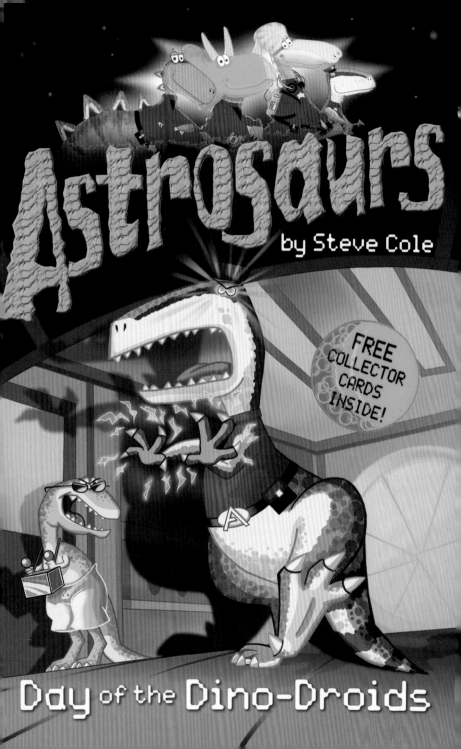

## Alarm Pterosaur

**Crew**

**FULL NAME:** Terri Alarmosaurus

**RANK:** Loudest screecher **AGE:** 53

**PLANET OF HATCHING:** Squawk Major

**DATA FILE:** Whenever danger looms, this pterosaur's beak is blowing out BEWARE!

**LIKES:** Swamp tea. Squawking. Getting in a flap

**DISLIKES:** People who talk quietly

**DSS RATING:** 9 – the *Sauropod* crew always know when they're in danger with this noisy dino-bird around!

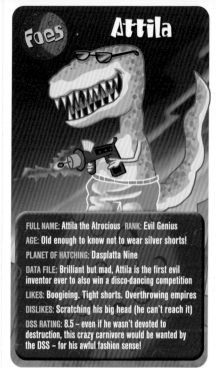

## Attila

**Foes**

**FULL NAME:** Attila the Atrocious **RANK:** Evil Genius

**AGE:** Old enough to know not to wear silver shorts!

**PLANET OF HATCHING:** Dasplatta Nine

**DATA FILE:** Brilliant but mad, Attila is the first evil inventor ever to also win a disco-dancing competition

**LIKES:** Boogieing. Tight shorts. Overthrowing empires

**DISLIKES:** Scratching his big head (he can't reach it)

**DSS RATING:** 8.5 – even if he wasn't devoted to destruction, this crazy carnivore would be wanted by the DSS – for his awful fashion sense!

## Dino-Droid Gipsy

**Foes**

**FULL NAME:** No name – only a serial number

**CLANK:** Whenever it moves **AGE:** Brand-new

**PLANET OF MANUFACTURE:** Ask Attila!

**DATA FILE:** Armed with miniature missiles, this devilish dino-droid is 100 per cent deadly!

**LIKES:** Blowing things up

**DISLIKES:** Anyone it's told to

**DSS RATING:** 9 – it looks like Gipsy, but it's really a mass of menacing machinery. AVOID AT ALL COSTS!

## Draxie

**Crew**

**FULL NAME:** Draxter McNaxter

**RANK:** Special Assistant to Admiral Rosso **AGE:** 26

**PLANET OF BIRTH:** Draconda

**DATA FILE:** A loyal, humble servant and ever so loyal to the DSS ... at least, that's what his mum says!

**LIKES:** Serving drinks. Staying out of trouble

**DISLIKES:** Power. He hates the stuff. Yuk! Power? No thanks! Ugh

**DSS RATING:** 5 – Draxie is one to watch – but maybe not for the right reasons ...

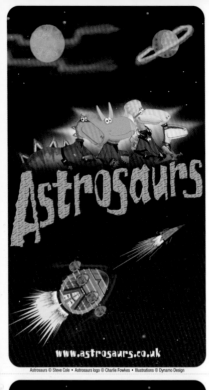

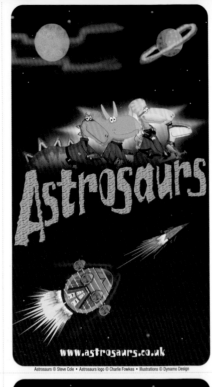

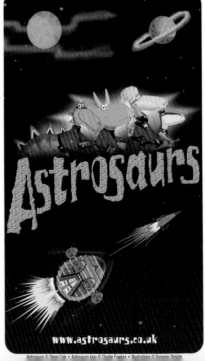

*Niamh*

Teggs is no ordinary dinosaur –
he's an **ASTROSAUR!** Captain of
the amazing spaceship DSS *Sauropod*,
he goes on dangerous missions and
fights evil – along with his faithful
crew, Gipsy, Arx and Iggy!

Collect all the **ASTROSAURS!**
Free collector cards in every book
for you to swap with your friends.
More cards available free from the
**ASTROSAURS!** website –
www.astrosaurs.co.uk

*Read all the adventures of*
*Teggs, Gipsy, Arx and Iggy!*

**BOOK ONE:**
RIDDLE OF THE RAPTORS

**BOOK TWO:**
THE HATCHING HORROR

**BOOK THREE:**
THE SEAS OF DOOM

**BOOK FOUR:**
THE MIND-SWAP MENACE

**BOOK FIVE:**
THE SKIES OF FEAR

**BOOK SIX:**
THE SPACE GHOSTS

*Coming soon*

**BOOK EIGHT:**
THE TERROR-BIRD TRAP

Find out more at www.astrosaurs.co.uk

# Astrosaurs

## DAY OF THE DINO-DROIDS

Steve Cole

*Illustrated by* Woody Fox

**RED FOX**

DAY OF THE DINO-DROIDS
A RED FOX BOOK 978 0 099 48797 5

First published in Great Britain by Red Fox,
an imprint of Random House Children's Books

This edition published 2006

5 7 9 10 8 6 4

Text copyright © Steve Cole, 2006
Cover illustration © Steve Richards/Dynamo Design
Illustrations copyright © Woody Fox, 2006
Map illustration © Charlie Fowkes 2006

The Random House Group Limited makes every effort to ensure that the
papers used in its books are made from trees that have been legally sourced
from well-managed and credibly certified forests. Our paper procurement
policy can be found at: www.randomhouse.co.uk/paper.htm

Typeset in Bembo Schoolbook by Palimpsest Book Production Limited,
Polmont, Stirlingshire

Red Fox Books are published by Random House Children's Books,
61–63 Uxbridge Road, London W5 5SA,
a division of The Random House Group Ltd

Addresses for companies within The Random House Group Limited can be
found at: www.randomhouse.co.uk/offices.htm

THE RANDOM HOUSE GROUP Limited Reg. No. 954009
www.**kids**at**randomhouse**.co.uk

A CIP catalogue record for this book is available from the British Library.

Printed in the UK by CPI Bookmarque, Croydon, CR0 4TD

*For Samuel Fleetwood*

# WARNING!

## THINK YOU KNOW ABOUT DINOSAURS?

### THINK AGAIN!

The dinosaurs . . .

Big, stupid, lumbering reptiles. Right?

All they did was eat, sleep and roar a bit. Right?

Died out millions of years ago when a big meteor struck the Earth. Right?

*Wrong!*

The dinosaurs weren't stupid. They may have had small brains, but they used them well. They had big thoughts and big dreams.

By the time the meteor hit, the last dinosaurs had already left Earth for ever. Some breeds had discovered how to travel through space as early as the Triassic period, and were already enjoying a new life among the stars. No one has found evidence of dinosaur technology yet. But the first fossil bones were only unearthed in 1822, and new finds are being made all the time.

The proof is out there, buried in the ground.

And the dinosaurs live on, way out in space, even now. They've settled down in a place they call the Jurassic Quadrant and over the last sixty-five million years they've gone on evolving.

The dinosaurs we'll be meeting are

part of a special group called the Dinosaur Space Service. Their job is to explore space, to go on exciting missions and to fight evil and protect the innocent!

These heroic herbivores are not just dinosaurs.

They are *astrosaurs*!

*NOTE: The following story has been translated from secret Dinosaur Space Service records. Earthling dinosaur names are used throughout, although some changes have been made for easy reading. There's even a guide to help you pronounce the dinosaur names at the back of the book.*

# THE CREW OF THE DSS SAUROPOD

**CAPTAIN
TEGGS STEGOSAUR**

**ARX ORANO,**
FIRST OFFICER

**GIPSY SAURINE,**
COMMUNICATIONS
OFFICER

**IGGY TOOTH,**
CHIEF ENGINEER

# Jurassic Quadrant

Ankylos

Steggos

Diplox

INDEPENDENT
DINOSAUR
ALLIANCE

vegetarian
sector

Squawk
Major

DSS
UNION OF
PLANETS

PTEROSAURIA

Tri System

Corytho

Lambeos

Trimuda

Creepus

Iguanos

Aqua Minor

OUTER SPACE

Geldos Cluster

Teerex
Major

Olympus

TYRANNOSAUR
TERRITORIES

carnivore

Planet Sixty

sector

Raptos

THEROPOD EMPIRE

Megalos

Cryptos

vegmeat

zone

(neutral space)

Atlantos

SEA REPTILE

SPACE

Pliosaur
Nurseries

Not to scale

# DAY OF THE
# DINO-DROIDS

## Chapter One

## THE TUNNEL IN SPACE

Captain Teggs was a very worried dinosaur.

Most days, he felt on top of the world – on top of *any* world. After all, he was in charge of the DSS *Sauropod*, the best ship in the whole Dinosaur Space Service. He had the finest, bravest crew any captain could hope for. And he even had a private larder crammed with three hundred types of delicious fern.

3

His life was one long exciting adventure in space – with just a spot of tummy-ache now and then.

But today, sat in the *Sauropod*'s control pit, he was worried. And with good reason. Admiral Rosso – the crusty old barosaurus in charge of the DSS – had disappeared.

"I've double-checked the admiral's movements," said Arx, Teggs's second-in-command, looking up from his controls. "He left in his private starship for a holiday on the planet Trimuda. But no one has seen or heard from him since."

Teggs nodded glumly. "And he was due back at DSS HQ yesterday!" He turned to his communications officer, a stripy hadrosaur named Gipsy. "Anything to report?"

"I've listened in to every message sent and every signal received in Trimuda's part of space over the last week." Gipsy put down her headphones with a sigh. "Nothing from Admiral Rosso."

Teggs chewed on some bracken. "I just hope we find him safe and well – and *fast*. The Pick-a-Planet meeting is due to be held in just three days, and if we're not back at DSS HQ with Admiral Rosso by then . . ."

"It could mean trouble," said Gipsy.

"Trouble with a capital T!" Teggs agreed.

New planets were discovered at the outer edges of the Jurassic Quadrant all the time. If they were found in the Vegetarian Sector, they were claimed by the plant-eaters. If they were found in the Carnivore Sector, they were taken by the meat-eaters. But any worlds discovered close to the Vegmeat Zone – the no-man's-land between the two dinosaur empires – were up for grabs. And each side wanted these worlds for themselves.

In olden times, there would be a big battle for each of the planets. But now, thanks to Admiral Rosso, things were different. Meat-eaters and plant-eaters alike gathered each year at DSS HQ for the Pick-a-Planet meeting. Here, the battles were fought with words, not weapons, and the planets were divided up evenly.

But Rosso was the only dinosaur trusted by both sides to play fair. Without him, the meeting could go dangerously wrong . . .

A loud bleep made the astrosaurs jump. The dimorphodon – the ship's fearless, fifty-strong flight crew – flapped over to perch at their positions, ready for anything.

Gipsy frowned at her controls. "It's Iggy," she said. "He's sent a code-two warning signal."

"*What?*" Teggs reared up in his control pit. Iggy was the *Sauropod*'s chief engineer. He was brilliant with all things mechanical. But a code-two warning signal meant he'd found a serious problem with the ship. "Put him on screen!"

Iggy's scowling, scaly face appeared on the scanner. "Captain, the engines seem to be playing up. I can't stop the ship slipping sideways through space!"

"*Sideways?*" Teggs frowned. "What do your controls say, Arx?"

Puzzled, Arx tried to scratch his head – but he couldn't reach, so a dimorphodon did it for him. "Iggy's right. We are drifting off-course."

"But why?" Gipsy wondered.

Arx looked very serious. "*Something* is pulling us towards it!"

"Let's see what's out there," said Teggs.

Gipsy whistled at the dimorphodon, and Iggy's face faded from the scanner to reveal the dark, sparkling wilderness of space.

"Nothing but a few stars and empty blackness!" Gipsy declared.

"It may be blackness, but I don't think it's empty." Arx turned to face his friends. "There's only one thing in space with the power to drag things towards it like this. A black hole!"

Teggs jumped out of his control pit.

9

"A black hole? But that's the most dangerous thing in the universe. Once it starts to suck you in, there's no escape!"

Gipsy's head-crest had flushed bright blue with alarm. "How come it's not marked on any of the star charts?"

"Perhaps it has just appeared," Arx suggested, checking his instruments.

"Well, that's very strange. This is no ordinary black hole. It seems to be the entrance to some kind of tunnel – a tunnel in space!"

"Then if it sucks us inside, who knows where we might come out," Gipsy hooted. "We could end up on the other side of the universe!"

"If we even survive the journey," said Teggs. "We must break free before it's too late!"

Another loud bleep startled them all – higher-pitched this time.

"A code-*one* warning," Gipsy gasped. "Iggy again!"

A dimorphodon bashed a button with his beak, and Iggy's face swam back into view on the scanner.

Beads of sweat sat upon his scaly brow.

"Captain, the dung-burners are working at full power but I still can't stop us slipping sideways! We're going faster and faster!"

"Iggy, listen," said Teggs. "There's some sort of tunnel in space out there and it's sucking us in! If we can't break free we're in big trouble. Can you boost the engines?"

The iguanodon gulped. "We'll need more dung," he said. "And fast!"

Teggs nodded. "Gipsy, quick! Tell Cook to serve up slimy seaweed and fruit chutney to everyone on board."

Iggy smiled grimly. "That should do it, sir."

Gipsy called the chef right away. But the ship had already started to shake, and the temperature was rising.

The alarm pterosaur started to squawk at the top of her lungs: "Danger! Red Alert! Finish your swamp tea! Hold on tight!"

A dreadful thought struck Teggs. "Do you think that Admiral Rosso's starship fell through this black-hole space-tunnel thing?"

"It seems very likely, Captain," Arx agreed, his horns drooping. "I'm afraid we may never find him now."

Suddenly, the ship rocked with a massive explosion. In the dim light, Iggy's sooty face appeared on the scanner.

"Forget the dung," he said bitterly. "The engines couldn't take the strain. They just blew up!"

"That means we will be sucked in even faster!" cried Arx.

The ship shook harder and started to spin. The lights dimmed. The whole flight deck grew burning hot. Even the ferns started to smoulder in the control pit. Teggs quickly ate them all before they could burst into flames.

He sighed, licking his lips. "That could be the last hot meal I ever eat!"

Then the ship lurched, and all the astrosaurs were thrown to the floor.

"We're picking up speed!" yelled Arx. "Ten seconds till we're sucked inside the space tunnel!"

"Hold on tight, everyone!" shouted Teggs. "I think we're about to find out how water feels when it goes down the plughole!"

Even as he spoke, the *Sauropod* hurtled headlong into the pit of blackness . . .

## Chapter Two

## SPAT INTO SPACE!

Arx and Gipsy scrambled into the control pit with Teggs. They clung onto one another as the screech of tearing metal echoed all around. The dimorphodon flocked together in the rafters. Then everything went black.

"We're travelling through the tunnel," gasped Arx. "Going faster than the speed of light!"

The *Sauropod* started to whizz around ever faster, like the astrosaurs were stuck in a washing machine at full spin. And then suddenly the ship was blown out the other end of the tunnel – a bit squashed, a bit squished, but still in one piece.

"We made it!" cried Teggs. Gipsy and
Arx cheered, while the dimorphodon
clapped their wings.

The ship stopped bucking. The
temperature started to fall. A few feeble
lights came on again.

"Quick," said Teggs, his brain still
spinning. "We must find out where
we are." Gipsy and Arx
hurried to
their posts.

"And I'll need a damage report," he
added. "Double quick!"

The doors to the flight deck slid open
and Iggy tottered inside. "Nothing's
working, Captain!"

"That's *triple* quick," Teggs muttered.

"Even the lift's broken. I had to take the stairs." Iggy stood there, covered in dirt and bruises, gasping for breath. "It was almost as bad as going through that space tunnel!"

"I'm afraid we have no way of knowing *where* we are, Captain," Arx announced, checking his own controls. "The *Sauropod*'s systems have been scrambled. We could be anywhere in the universe."

"Even somewhere in the Carnivore Sector," said Teggs gravely. "Helpless!"

Then suddenly the scanner screen buzzed into life. The picture was blurry, speckled with static. But the astrosaurs recognized the view at once. It was a massive space station, made up of several vast towers linked by metal walkways. A long pole, bristling with aerials and satellite dishes, stuck out from below.

"It's DSS Headquarters!" gasped Teggs. "The space tunnel spat us out on our own doorstep!"

"We're home!" Gipsy whooped for joy.

Iggy did a funky victory dance and the dimorphodon flapped about him, merrily cheeping.

But Arx was just staring at the scanner. "I don't believe it," he said.

"The chances of finding ourselves back here are microscopic!"

"This is DSS HQ calling the *Sauropod*." The voice crackled over the ship's battered speakers. "Captain Teggs, can you hear me?"

Gipsy flicked some switches. "Putting you through, Captain, with the last of our power."

Teggs cleared his throat. "This is Teggs. Our ship's been badly damaged and we need help. We were out searching for Admiral Rosso when—"

"Searching for me, Teggs?" The booming voice over the speakers was unmistakable. "But I'm right here!"

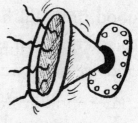

The image of HQ on the scanner was replaced by a bespectacled barosaurus, looking kindly down at them.

"Admiral Rosso!" beamed Teggs.
"You're back safe! But how . . . ?"

Rosso shook his little head. "All in good time. I'll have the *Sauropod* towed to safety. Then you can come aboard and we can swap stories. Rosso out."

The scanner screen went dark.

Teggs beamed at his friends. "All's well that ends well," he said happily. "We'll soon have the ship repaired and be on our way. I think I'll go round and tell the crew in person."

"I'll come with you," said Gipsy, and Iggy followed on behind.

But Arx remained, deep in thought. Something in his sturdy old bones told him that the danger wasn't over yet — not for any of them.

## Chapter Three

### INTRUDER!

Within the hour the *Sauropod* was safely docked with DSS HQ. While the crew made repairs to the ship, Teggs, Arx, Iggy and Gipsy were invited to Admiral Rosso's office. The walls and floor were thick with vines and vegetables, and Teggs wasted no time filling his stomach.

A small dinosaur with a knobbly
back entered the office balancing a
tray of cool swampshakes and
grasswater on his back. A flashy velvet
sash was tied around his waist.

"This is Draxie," Rosso announced.
"My special assistant. He's
a dracopelta."

The astrosaurs
said hello as
Draxie shuffled
about on all
fours, passing round the drinks.

"So tell us what happened, Admiral
Rosso," said Teggs, draining his
grasswater with a contented burp. "Did
you get sucked into the space tunnel,
like us?"

"Not a bit of it, Teggs," boomed the
old barosaurus, stretching out his long
neck. "I changed my mind about going
to Trimuda. I went fishing on Aqua
Twenty-three instead!"

"Everyone was very worried about you, sir," said Arx. "Especially with the Pick-a-Planet meeting coming up."

"Yes, sorry about that," Rosso chortled. "I was enjoying myself so much that I lost all track of time. I got back not long after you'd started to search for me. Sent you a message to call off the hunt – did it not reach you?"

Gipsy frowned. "Strange. I thought I'd listened in on every single message zinging through that part of space."

"Perhaps this mysterious space tunnel sucked up the message before it could reach you, miss," Draxie suggested, offering her another drink.

"It's an incredible coincidence that we were spat out right here," said Arx.

"Has anything else curious arrived on your doorstep lately?"

"Not that we know of, sir," said Draxie.

"We should find that space tunnel and seal it off," Rosso told him. "Can't afford any funny business with the Pick-a-Planet meeting coming up."

"I'll lead the mission if you like, sir," Teggs offered.

"No, no, no." Rosso shook his head. "You deserve a rest after what you've been through. All of you!"

Gipsy stretched. "I guess I *am* quite tired."

"Me too!" yawned Iggy.

"Take them to the guest rooms, Draxie," said Rosso. "We can talk again later."

So the astrosaurs followed the little dracopelta out of the admiral's office and into the airy corridor.

Teggs paused to chomp on some jungle vines. "I haven't been back to DSS HQ for ages," he remarked. "The old place looks a bit different."

"We are busy redecorating, sir," said Draxie. "Getting ready for the Pick-a-Planet meeting."

"Not many people about, either," Iggy observed.

"All crew not vital to the running of HQ have been sent away," Draxie told him. "Our visiting VIDs don't like crowds."

"VIDs?" asked Gipsy, puzzled.

Draxie nodded. "Very Important Dinosaurs, of course!"

They took the lift down to level nine.

"Your room is through here, Miss Saurine," said Draxie, gesturing to a sliding door. "The rest of you have rooms on level eight."

"Sleep well," Teggs told Gipsy. "See you in the morning."

Gipsy saluted, and watched them go.
Then she opened the door. The room was
large and softly lit. A lovely bed made
from reeds and lilies stood in one corner.

But just as she stepped inside, a
bright crimson light filled the room
and started flashing on and off. Gipsy
felt very strange – like her brain had
got pins and needles. Dazzled, she
closed her eyes.

When she opened them again, the
light had gone.

"Funny," she muttered. "I wonder what caused that."

Then she noticed a funny smell in the air . . .

"Meat!" she breathed. "Ugh! I can smell meat!"

Baffled, Gipsy sniffed her way around the room. There was a large cupboard in the corner. The closer she got, the stronger the hateful smell became . . .

Until suddenly the door burst open – to reveal a monstrous carnivore hiding inside!

Gipsy jumped back in alarm from the drooling dinosaur. He looked like a T. rex, only smaller and chunkier, and with even longer teeth. He wore a horrid pair of silver shorts. And he held a strange-looking ray gun in his claws.

"I've been waiting for you, Gipsy Saurine," hissed the dinosaur. "I hope my little flashing lights didn't distress you ..."

"Not as much as your shorts!" said Gipsy. Then her eyes narrowed. "So. *You* made the lights go funny? Why?"

He snapped his jaws. "I have taken something from you. Something I needed that only *you* could give me."

"I'll give you a jab on the snout if you don't give yourself up right now!" said Gipsy, raising her hooves.

The carnivore trained his gun on her.

Gipsy scowled. "Don't you know it's bad manners to shoot someone before you've introduced yourself?"

"I'm a daspletosaurus," rasped the intruder. "We *have* no manners!"

"When it comes to meat-eaters with no fashion sense, neither do I!" Gipsy swung round her tail and knocked the gun from his hand.

"Whoops! Butter-claws!"

The daspletosaurus growled crossly and picked up his gun. Then he opened his fearsome jaws and lunged for her.

Gipsy ducked aside and ran from the room.

She spoke quickly into her wrist communicator. "Captain Teggs, this is Gipsy. There's a carnivore intruder on board! A daspletosaurus – armed and dangerous." She heard heavy footsteps pounding after her, and a beam of energy sizzled past her ear. "*Very* dangerous! He was hiding in my room, and now he's chasing me on level nine. Help!"

Teggs's voice crackled over the tiny speaker. "Hang in there, Gipsy. We're on our way!"

Gipsy ran faster through the maze of corridors. She had trained at DSS HQ for years, so she knew all the short cuts and the best places to hide. But lots of corridors seemed to be closed for redecorating, cutting off her escape routes. And from the sound of his heavy footsteps, the daspletosaurus was still close behind.

Then, with
a gasp of
horror, Gipsy
turned a
corner and
found herself
facing a
dead end –
a blank wall
with a huge
air vent built
into it.

"I don't
remember this
being here!" she
muttered, scrabbling at the metal grille.
If she could quickly climb inside and
hide . . .

But Gipsy was too late. The
daspletosaurus came up behind her and
grabbed her! She stamped on his foot
and pulled free of his grip. But she had
nowhere to run.

"Curse these feeble forearms," said the carnivore, sighing. "Even weight-lifting doesn't help!" He flexed his minuscule muscles and shimmied in his silvery shorts. "Still, at least you have saved me the trouble of carrying you here. Now I have you right where I want you."

"You'd better run while you can, you disco disaster!" Gipsy told him bravely. "My friends are on their way."

The daspletosaurus chuckled. "They will be too late to stop me!"

He raised the strange-looking gun, and fired . . .

## Chapter Four

## A MECHANICAL MENACE?

Teggs lumbered down the corridors of
DSS HQ at top speed – he may have
been an eight-ton stegosaurus but he
was nimble with it. He found Gipsy
first, just ahead of Arx, Iggy and
Draxie. She was lying flat on her back
with her legs in the air,
in front of the air vent.

"Gipsy!" he cried. "What happened? Are you all right?"

Her eyes flicked open. "I'm fine, Captain. Is anything wrong?"

He frowned. "Yes – your memory! You told me you were being chased by a crazy carnivore!"

"Did I?" Gipsy got up from the floor. She looked very confused. "Sorry, sir. I must have been dreaming."

"In that case, how come you're here and not in your bed?" asked Teggs.

She shrugged. "I guess I must have sleepwalked."

"Sleep*ran*, more like!" Teggs turned to Draxie. "You'd better check the whole place for intruders."

"I'm on the case, sir." Draxie pulled a round green gadget from the sash beneath his belly.

"My life-sign scanner will soon show up any intruders."

"How?" asked Arx.

"It knows the brainwaves and heartbeat of all DSS crew members on board," Draxie explained. "If it finds someone it doesn't recognize – someone who shouldn't be here – it'll start to beep."

But the machine stayed silent.

"You see?" Draxie showed Teggs the gadget. "No intruders on board. Miss Saurine *was* dreaming."

"Maybe not . . ." Arx was studying the air vent behind Gipsy. "Captain, this grille has been opened recently."

Iggy had a look too.

"He's right. These screws are loose."

"You two are the ones with loose screws," teased Gipsy. "I'll bet I tried to get inside the vent in my sleep. That's all."

"Well, what about these scratches?" said Arx. Teggs moved closer to see for himself. There were deep score-marks in the metal around the grille. "*You* couldn't have made them, Gipsy. Your hooves aren't sharp enough."

"But a carnivore's claws *are*," said Teggs.

Gipsy moved forwards to take a closer look – but then she slipped and fell into Iggy's arms. With a gasp, he fell to the floor, squashed beneath her.

"Have you been secretly eating all the ship's pies?" he groaned. "You're heavier than you look!"

"Cheek!" said Gipsy, quickly scrambling back up.

"You slipped in some sort of *oil*, Gipsy," said Arx, peering down at a small yellow puddle. "Where did that come from?"

Iggy dipped his finger in the oil and sniffed it. "That's Robotix Motor Oil!" he announced. "I got through tons of the stuff when I worked in the DSS solar workshops – I'd recognize it anywhere. And there's only one thing that runs on Robotix – robots!"

"Robots!" cried Arx. "Of course!"

Teggs frowned. "What's on your mind?"

"Gipsy told us she saw a daspletosaurus, but Draxie's device can't find its heartbeat or brainwaves," said Arx. "So maybe, just maybe, this intruder is a *robot* — a machine!"

Iggy stared at him. "A clockwork carnivore?"

"It's possible," Teggs agreed. "A robot doesn't have a heart — only a motor."

Arx nodded excitedly. "And it has a computer for a brain — so it would *never* show up on Draxie's scanner!"

"But DSS HQ has top-level security, sir," Draxie protested. "No one can get in here without us knowing — least of all a mechanical meat-guzzler!" He sighed. "But with the Pick-a-Planet meeting so close, I suppose we can't take any chances."

"Exactly," said Teggs. "Organize a full search of the whole station."

"Yes, sir," said Draxie. "Oh, and, Mr Arx, perhaps you should tell Admiral Rosso about your suspicions."

"Good thinking," said Teggs. "Iggy, go with him. I'll walk Gipsy back to her room, then I'll come and join you."

"Yes, sir!" Iggy saluted – flicking a blob of oil from his claw as he did so. *Splat!* It hit Gipsy in the eye. "Oh, sorry!"

But to Teggs's surprise she didn't even blink. "That's all right, Iggy. Goodnight."

Iggy grinned and waved. "*Oil* see you later!"

Gipsy didn't even smile. She simply turned and walked away.

Teggs frowned. Gipsy was acting oddly. He could only suppose she was more shaken by her close encounter than she liked to let on. But if there *was* a robot dinosaur on the loose . . . how come she didn't remember?

As Arx and Iggy approached Admiral Rosso's office, a pterosaur flapped down the corridor towards them. "The admiral's not in his office," she squawked. "He's in Room 202."

"Room 202?" Arx frowned. "That's a

workshop down on the second level, isn't it? What would Admiral Rosso be doing there?"

"Making something?" Iggy suggested. "Perhaps it's his hobby."

They took the lift down to level two. It seemed to Arx that almost *every* room was closed for redecorating. "I hope they finish repainting before the Pick-a-Planet meeting starts," he said as they stopped outside Room 202.

Suddenly the door slid open. "Admiral Rosso?" called Iggy.

No one answered. Arx and Iggy went inside. The workshop was filled with smoke and sparks and the whine of machines – and an eerie, bright crimson light, flashing on and off, on and off . . .

It made them both feel funny. Arx felt like his head was full of fog. Iggy felt like there were earwigs partying between his ears. But then the crimson light faded and they pressed on in search of the admiral.

"Look over there!" Iggy glimpsed movement through the smoke. "That must be him. I wonder what he's making."

He pointed to one corner, where someone was hammering at a large metal object. It was long, maybe eight metres, and full of wires and motors. Large steel sails ran in a row along its top. A gleaming metal tail whirred from side to side, tipped with iron spikes.

"It looks like a metal stegosaurus!"
Arx breathed. "It must be a statue of
Captain Teggs."

"Statue?" Iggy shook his head.
"Looks more like a robot to me!"

"Admiral?" called Arx. "May we
speak with you?"

Then both he and Iggy gasped as a
large, menacing shape came into view
from behind the gleaming sculpture. It
wasn't Admiral Rosso at all – it was a
daspletosaurus, just as Gipsy had
described!

The carnivore was wearing dark glasses and a pair of awful silver shorts. In one hand he held a welding torch, and in the other, a strange sort of gun . . .

Iggy gulped. "That thing doesn't look like a robot to me!"

"Welcome to my lair, gentlemen," the daspletosaurus hissed. "I hope you didn't mind my little flashing lights. Thanks to them, I have taken from you all that I need!"

"Oh yeah?" growled Iggy, clenching his scaly fists. "Well, allow me to give you something extra!"

He and Arx charged bravely forwards
– but the carnivore quickly zapped
them with his ray gun. They slumped
to the floor.

The daspletosaurus chuckled and
wiggled his silver tail. Then he turned
to his creepy robot stegosaur. "That's
your friends dealt with, Captain Teggs,"
he whispered. "And soon, it will be *your*
turn!"

## Chapter Five

## DEADLY DISCOVERY

Teggs took Gipsy back to her room to rest. He had a good look around, but there was no sign that another dinosaur had ever been there. *Could* she have imagined the whole thing? Had the oil been spilled by a robotic vacuum cleaner? Were the scratches by the air vent left by clumsy decorators?

He went up to Admiral Rosso's office to join Arx and Iggy. But, to his surprise, they weren't there.

"No one's come to see me," Rosso told him.

"Is my pterosaur outside? She normally makes all my appointments."

"No. She must have popped out." Teggs sighed. "Why does everyone keep disappearing around here?"

Rosso sat down behind his vast wooden desk. "Why did Arx and Iggy want to see me, anyway?"

Teggs explained what had happened to Gipsy, and about Arx's robot theory. But Rosso just laughed.

"My dear Teggs, that's a bit far-fetched, isn't it?" He snorted. "Dino-droids, here in HQ? They could never get on board!"

Teggs uprooted a small tree and chewed on it moodily. "Maybe not, sir, but I've got Draxie searching the station just in case."

Rosso nodded. "I suppose that with

the Pick-a-Planet meeting coming up, we can't be too careful. Don't want anything to go wrong after all our careful planning, do we? Keep me informed!"

"Yes, sir." Teggs tugged the last leaves from the sapling, spat out a twig and saluted. As he left the office, his wrist communicator beeped.

"Captain Teggs? This is Draxie. My search party of ankylosaurs have checked levels one to five so far. No trace of intruders."

"Any sign of Arx and Iggy?"

Draxie sounded puzzled. "Aren't they in Admiral Rosso's office?"

"Not unless they were hiding under the table!" joked Teggs. "Well, keep up the search — and be careful. Teggs out!"

He set off along the corridor. HQ was eerily quiet with so few people around. Teggs raised his communicator to  his beak. "Arx? Iggy? Where are you?"

There was no reply.

Maybe they went to get something from their rooms, thought Teggs, getting into the lift. He pressed the button for level eight. When the doors opened, he saw Gipsy standing there.

"Hello," said Teggs, slightly puzzled. "I thought you were resting."

"I've come to take you to see Arx and Iggy," Gipsy told him.

"You have?" Teggs grinned. "Great! Where are they?"

"Waiting in a workshop on level two," she said. "Come with me— *Oops!*"

Gipsy suddenly skidded on something. With a squawk and a crash, she banged her head on the wall.

"Are you all right?" asked Teggs. "What did you slip on?"

"Nothing," she said.

"It's oil again!" Teggs realized. "Where did that come from?" But then he saw a strange, slimy stain on Gipsy's waist. "There's more of it there! Gipsy, have you been taking a bath in the stuff?"

"Don't be silly, sir," she said, turning away.

And as she did, Teggs's eyes widened. "Gipsy, where you banged your head on the wall – it's left a dent!"

Gipsy shrugged. "Must be a weak wall."

"I'm not talking about the wall!" said Teggs. "*The dent is in your head!*"

Gipsy turned to face him. He could see now that the stain on her uniform was caused by a steady *drip-drip-drip* of yellow liquid. She was leaking! It was her *own* oil she had slipped in!

"You're not the real Gipsy at all, are you?" said Teggs grimly. "You're a robot. A dino-droid!"

Even as he spoke, Gipsy's eyes turned red and started to spin. A door opened up in her head-crest — to reveal a miniature missile launcher.

It was aiming straight at Teggs!

## Chapter Six

## ATTACK OF THE DINO-DROIDS!

"What have you done with the real Gipsy?" Teggs demanded. "Where is she?"

"Don't worry," rasped the dino-droid Gipsy. "You will soon be joining her!"

"Not likely!" said Teggs, and before she could fire her missile he whacked her metal hip with his tail.

She staggered to one side, and the drip of oil became a spurt – soon the corridor's floor was slippier than a greased-up banana skin. Teggs turned and ran, but when the dino-droid tried to follow him she slipped and slid about like an elephant on ice-skates.

"Come back!" she roared, falling flat on her face with a crash. "Come back! My masters want you!"

"Then they'll have to do better than that!" Teggs shouted back to her. He ran down a side corridor – and grinned with relief.

Arx and Iggy were bundling round the corner towards him.

"Guys! Thank goodness I've found you!" Teggs skidded to a halt, suddenly uncertain. "Er, it *is* you, isn't it?"

Iggy looked hurt. "Of course it's us. But is that really *you*?"

"I'm real all right," said Teggs. "Where have you been?"

"We were lured into a trap," said Arx.
"But we got away. Gipsy was right –
there *is* a crazy carnivore on board.
He's been hiding in a workshop on
level two. And he's building a
dino-droid in the shape of a
stegosaurus!"

"He must want to replace the real
me with a robot," Teggs realized. "Just
like he's done with Gipsy!"

"Gipsy, a dino-droid?" gasped Iggy.

Teggs nodded. "I think the carnivore
took the real Gipsy away through that
air vent, and dumped a robot in her
place – scratching the cover as he did so."

59

"That explains why she felt so heavy when I picked her up," said Iggy. "But she — I mean, *it* — was so life-like!"

"I know," said Teggs. "I only realized the truth when I saw she was leaking Robotix Oil."

"So it wasn't a mechanical *carnivore* that left those drips behind," Arx realized. "It was the fake Gipsy!"

Teggs heard a loud clonking noise from the main corridor. "And it sounds like she's finding her feet again. Let's get out of here. We must warn Draxie and Admiral Rosso!"

"No need to warn *me*, Teggs!" boomed the admiral's voice as he lumbered round the corner. "When I heard all that crashing about, I came to investigate." He looked very serious. "What can we do? Who can we trust? Maybe *Draxie* is one of them!"

Teggs stared in alarm. "Your own special assistant, a dino-droid?"

"Why not?" said Arx calmly. "After all . . . *we* are."

"That's not funny," said Teggs.

But then he saw that Arx's eyes had turned red. They were spinning around like electric fireworks – and the tips of his horns fell away to reveal three threatening nozzles!

Iggy's eyes were spinning too. Red sparks of energy crackled around his claws . . .

"Good grief, they really *are* dino-droids!" cried Teggs. "Run, Admiral! I'll hold them off!"

"I'm not leaving you, Teggs," said Rosso. Then he smiled as his *own* eyes began to spin. "I'm going to take you to my masters!"

"You've tricked me," groaned Teggs. "All of you!"

"We kept you talking until other dino-droids came to help us," the robotic Rosso agreed. "Now you are trapped!"

Suddenly Rosso swung his head like a wrecking ball in Teggs's direction. Teggs jumped clear just in time, and it smashed into the wall. Iggy shot sparks from his claws, missing Teggs by millimetres. Arx shot a spray of smelly gas from his nozzles, but Teggs held his

breath, turned and ran back the way
he had come.

But he soon realized the Rosso-droid
was right. It wasn't just a limping
dino-droid Gipsy he had to deal with
now. Four ankylosaurs with spinning
eyes were trudging towards him, two
on either side of her. Together they
completely blocked the corridor.

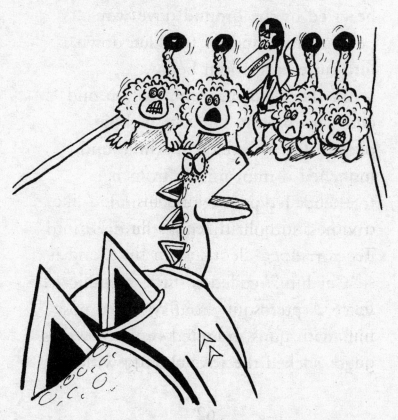

"I can't go forwards and I can't go back," Teggs realized as the Rosso-droid and its mechanical mates came lumbering round the corner. "So since dinosaurs can't fly, I'll just have to go *down*!"

With that, Teggs brought his tail crashing against the floor beside him with all his strength. "Geronimoooooo!" he cried as the ground gave way beneath him and he tumbled down into an empty room below.

But there was no time to stop and catch his breath. The Gipsy-droid peered down through the hole and launched a mini-missile from her forehead. Teggs dived aside and smashed straight through the door into the corridor.

"Get him!" called a shrill, metallic voice. A pterosaur-droid swooped past him with guns mounted on both wings. Teggs socked the fake flapper with his

tail and it spiralled into a wall, exploding with a loud squawk. But soon more pterosaur-droids were zooming round the corner, eyes flashing red, firing their wing-guns.

Teggs turned and galloped away. "I've got to get back to the *Sauropod*," he muttered. "With the rest of the ship's crew to help me, I might just stand a chance against these dratted dino-droids— *Whoops!*"

He sped round the corner at top speed, only to find a dead end up ahead with a large air vent in it – like the place where they had found the Gipsy-droid.

Teggs couldn't stop in time. BOING! *KA-KRANNG!* He crashed into the grille so hard it buckled around his head and clattered to the floor.

Dazed, he scrambled back up. Three of the pterosaur-droids were flying straight at him.

He grabbed the grille with his beak and threw it at them like a metal frisbee. It hit two of the droids and made them blow up – scorching the bottom of the third. With a squawk it flew straight up and conked itself on the ceiling.

Safe for a few moments, Teggs turned
to the air vent. If he went through it
into the duct, he might find a way to
reach the docking bay where the
*Sauropod* stood waiting. He might even
find the real Gipsy somewhere on the
way.

Or he *might* find himself in the heart
of the carnivore's lair. He knew now
that it wasn't a robot – it was real.

Cautiously, Teggs squeezed into the
vent and shuffled forwards into the
menacing maze of pipes . . .

## Chapter Seven

## THE TRAP

The pipes were dark
and scary. Stale warm
air gusted through
them. They were also
a tight squeeze for
Teggs's tummy. He
wished he hadn't eaten
that extra sapling in
Rosso's office.

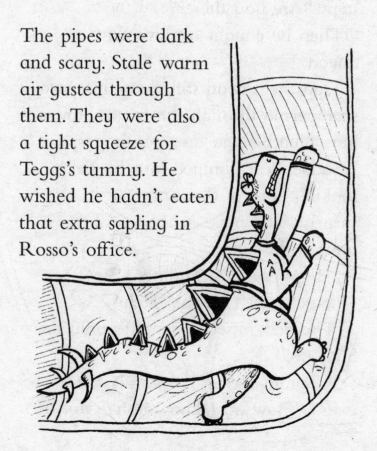

How long had he spent in this gloomy metal world? Teggs had lost all track of time. But he knew he couldn't turn back — there was no room to turn round, for one thing. So he pressed onwards through the murky tunnels.

"Gipsy?" he whispered every few steps. "Are you there?"

Then he caught a movement up ahead.

Teggs held dead still. Something was scampering through the tunnels towards him, breathing in fast, frantic gasps.

Suddenly it bumped into his belly, making both of them cry out in surprise. The noise echoed eerily around the pipes.

"Help!" came a familiar voice. "Please don't hurt me! Help!"

"Draxie!" hissed Teggs. "It's only me. Shut up!"

"Captain Teggs?" Draxie backed away. "How do I know you're not a

70

dino-droid?"

"How do I know *you're* not?" Teggs countered. "Everyone *else* is around here!" He pressed his communicator and its tiny bulb lit up the dracopelta with a weak yellow glow.

Draxie looked sweaty and scared. "I'm flesh and blood all right, sir! See this?" He turned his scaly cheek and Teggs could see he had a nasty scratch there. "I got this from a pterosaur-droid on level four. This duct was the only place I could think of to hide."

"Snap," said Teggs. "I don't suppose you've found Gipsy anywhere in here?"

"No, sir. Has she been turned into a droid too?"

Teggs nodded. "Together with Rosso, Arx and Iggy. We could be the only real astrosaurs left on this station!"

"Then we must get help, sir," said Draxie. "Send a signal to all other DSS ships in the area. Perhaps we could hide on the *Sauropod*?"

"Do you know the way there?" asked Teggs urgently.

"I think so," said Draxie. "Follow me."

Teggs squeezed through the duct with new hope in his big, thumping heart. Draxie was smaller and could move much faster, so he kept scouting ahead to make sure they were going the right way.

"I think it's just through here, sir," Draxie whispered. "You stay put. I'll check that it's safe."

Teggs waited in the darkness as Draxie's footsteps faded away. He heard a distant, rusty squeak as the dracopelta opened the air vent's grille.

And then he heard a scream.

"Draxie?" Teggs shouted. "Are you OK?"

"They've got me, sir!" Draxie cried. "The dino-droids! They were hiding here, waiting for me!" he yelped. "Go back, sir! Save yourself!"

Teggs shook his head. "I can't just leave you!" Gritting his teeth he thundered along the pipeline and burst out through the grille with a roar of anger. If he could only fight his way through to the safety of the *Sauropod* . . .

But the ship was nowhere to be seen. This wasn't the docking bay. It was some kind of workshop.

And Draxie wasn't being held prisoner by the dino-droids. He was standing beside a nasty-looking daspletosaurus in nasty silver shorts who was holding a very nasty-looking gun.

"Don't move, Captain," said the carnivore, smiling. "My name is Attila. Attila the Atrocious!"

"Named after your dress sense, I bet," said Teggs.

Attila ignored him. "I am ruler of all robots and master of mechanical monsters – deadly dino-droids a speciality."

"For someone with such titchy arms you've got a big head, Attila," growled Teggs.

"I have big *teeth* too," said Attila, snapping his jaws. "So watch it!"

"So much for the fabulous Captain Teggs Stegosaur." Draxie laughed. "I fooled you completely – 'sir'!"

Teggs nodded crossly. "All that nonsense about scanning for the intruder's heartbeat and brainwaves. You faked it, didn't you? You knew this carnivore was on board all the time!"

"Yup!" said Draxie smugly. "But you're flesh and blood! A plant-eater!" Teggs protested.

"Why are you helping atrocious Attila? I don't understand!"

Draxie smirked. "That's because your brain is the size of an unripe acorn."

"I can't argue with you there," Teggs admitted.

"Enough talk," hissed Attila. "It's time my collection of dino-droid astrosaurs was complete!"

"No way," said Teggs firmly. "You're not turning *me* into one of your pet robots!"

But even as he spoke, dazzling crimson lights shone down from the ceiling. They flashed on and off, on and off. Teggs shut his eyes and gasped.

His skull started itching on the inside. It felt like his brain was filled with tickly termites waving feather dusters.

Then the sinister glow faded away.

Teggs groaned. "You may be dressed for a disco, Attila, but your light show needs some work!"

"The time for joking is over, Captain," said Draxie. "We have no further use for you."

Attila nodded. "I have taken all that I need."

"Not quite. Now you can take *this*!" bellowed Teggs. He broke into a charge, whirling his spiky tail around his head.

But Attila did a fancy disco twirl, raised his gun and opened fire. Teggs took a direct hit. He staggered backwards and crashed into something.

It was a large, orange-brown stegosaurus. An exact double of himself! Teggs's mirror image smiled nastily, and brought its tail down on his head.

CRACK!

Everything went black.

## Chapter Eight

## THE EVIL PLOT

When Teggs awoke, he was lying face down on the floor in a damp, grimy room, tied up with chains. "Oh, my head!" he groaned.
"Where am I?"

"In hot water," said Gipsy, from behind him.

"Along with the rest of us," Iggy added.

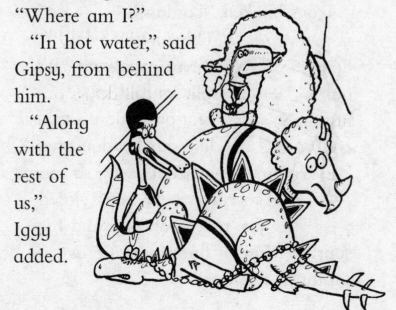

79

Teggs rolled over, expecting to find himself face-to-face with dino-droids. But in an instant he knew that these bruised and battered astrosaurs were the real thing. Gipsy, Arx, Iggy and Admiral Rosso – they might have been trussed up like prehistoric turkeys, but they still smiled at him warmly.

"What a disaster." Teggs sighed. "I can't believe that Attila the Atrocious has actually taken over DSS HQ!"

"Not yet he hasn't," said Gipsy.

Teggs blinked. "Pardon?"

"This *isn't* DSS HQ!" Rosso explained. "It's just an old space station done up to *look* like our headquarters!"

"That's why so many corridors have been closed for 'redecoration'," said Iggy sourly. "Most of the rooms are as grotty as this one!"

"But it looked *exactly* like HQ from the outside!" Teggs protested. "We saw it on board the *Sauropod*!"

"That was just an image they beamed onto your broken scanner," said Rosso sadly. "They tricked me in the same way."

"You see, Attila created the space tunnel himself," Arx went on. "Somehow it works like a short cut through space. It sucked us all in and then spat us out on the doorstep of this fake HQ . . . deep in the Tyrannosaur Territories!"

"That *really* sucks," said Teggs.

Gipsy nodded sadly. "And because our instruments were broken, we couldn't tell where we really were."

Teggs nodded. "How come you know all this?"

"Because Attila is a big show-off and keeps gloating about how clever he is," said Gipsy. "And Draxie is even worse!"

Rosso nodded. "He used to work at the DSS. But he was kicked out long ago – for making sneaky deals with carnivores!"

"Now it looks like he's made his sneakiest deal *ever*," said Iggy gloomily.

"But just what are the two of them planning?" Teggs wondered.

Just then, the door creaked open. Attila and Draxie marched inside, accompanied by dino-droids of Arx, Gipsy, Iggy and Teggs.

Teggs gulped. It was a creepy feeling, looking at perfect copies of himself and his crew.

"We have come to say goodbye," said Draxie.

Teggs raised his eyebrows. "And to gloat about your master plan, I suppose."

Draxie looked shifty. "Er, maybe."

"Go on, then," said Teggs. "Tell us all how clever you are."

"I am not *clever*," Attila declared. "I am a *genius*! You can see for yourself, my dino-droids are perfect – because I borrowed bits from each of you to build them!"

Teggs frowned. "Eh?"

"Of course," groaned Arx. "That flashing crimson light we saw . . ."

"I was simply taking a snapshot," chortled Attila. "A snapshot of your *minds*! All your thoughts and memories were captured and copied and fed into the dino-droids' computer brains – so they behave just like *you* do."

"So that's why you brought us halfway across the Jurassic Quadrant," breathed Teggs.

Draxie smiled. "We also needed to test out our Rosso-droid. We knew that if it could fool all of you it could fool *anyone*!"

"And now our dino-droids will travel in the *Sauropod* to the *real* DSS HQ," said Attila. "Captain Teggs and his crew returning home with Admiral Rosso – all safe and sound."

"Oh, I get it," said Teggs. "You want to mess up the Pick-a-Planet meeting!"

"Our Rosso-droid will pick a fight with the raptor generals," said Attila. "This will start a war between the Theropod Empire and the entire Vegetarian Sector."

"The DSS will send its best ships into battle," Draxie went on. "All hopes will be pinned on brave Captain Teggs and his crew in the *Sauropod* . . ."

"But imagine the outcry when the *Sauropod* opens fire on the other ships in the DSS fleet. When it blows up DSS HQ!" Attila's long, sharp teeth glinted in a smile. "When Teggs joins forces with the raptors and helps them destroy the Vegetarian Sector!"

"I would never do that!" spluttered Teggs.

"But my Teggs dino-droid *will*," crowed the carnivore, shaking his booty in excitement. "You and your crew will become known as the most-hated traitors in history!"

"You flimsy-armed fiend!" cried Rosso. "What's in it for you?"

"When the Vegetarian Sector and the Theropod Empire have battled each other to a standstill, the tyrannosaurs will declare war on them *both*," Attila cackled. "They will be easy to beat – especially when the *Sauropod* switches to *our* side. Tyrannosaurs will rule the entire Jurassic Quadrant – and *I* shall be their emperor!"

"And *I* shall be the emperor's most loyal servant," added Draxie. "With a mini-empire all of my own."

Gipsy's head-crest turned scarlet with rage. "You disgusting dracopelta!" she cried, hurling herself at Draxie. She bashed him with her bill and tore off his velvet sash in her fury, before her dino-droid double threw her aside.

"I think it's time we left," said Draxie, crossly picking up his sash. "The *Sauropod* is now fully repaired. We shall take it and travel to the Pick-a-Planet meeting."

"And everyone will think that clever Captain Teggs has succeeded in his mission once again," said Attila. "If they only knew . . ."

"You can't just leave us here to rot!" cried Iggy.

"Can too!" Draxie retorted. "And we are leaving dino-droid guards outside this door. If you try to escape, they will destroy you. Bye-eeee!"

With that, the two devilish dinosaurs and their dino-droids left the room. Teggs caught a glimpse of fierce ankylosaur-droids and robot pterosaurs with red spinning eyes lurking outside.

Then the door slammed shut – sealing them inside for good.

## Chapter Nine

## ONE LAST HOPE

"We've got to stop those monsters!" cried Teggs. "If we don't, the Jurassic Quadrant is doomed!"

Rosso nodded. "First, we have to get out of *here*."

"But how?" Arx sighed.

"Wait a minute," said Teggs. He had noticed something round and green on the floor beside Gipsy. "What's that?"

She looked down. "It's Draxie's life-sign scanner. It must have fallen out when I yanked off his sash."

Rosso stretched his neck to take a look. "This thing picks up heartbeats and brainwaves, doesn't it? Don't see how that can help us."

"Wait a minute," breathed Iggy. "Perhaps it *can*! If I can just free my hands . . ."

"Use the armour plates on my back to cut through your ropes," Teggs suggested. "They should be sharp enough."

Iggy hopped over to Teggs and soon freed himself. He took the back off the scanner and started fiddling with the wires. "Can I borrow your communicator, Captain?"

Teggs let him pull it off his wrist. "What's your plan, Iggy?"

"I reckon that if I can wire these two gadgets together in just the right way, I can make a sort of jamming device," he explained.

Arx beamed. "That's a brilliant idea, Iggy!"

"Let's hope it works," said Iggy, his claws a blur as he set to work.

Teggs and the others waited in tense silence.

Finally, Iggy turned on his strange electronic creation. *Screeeeeeeeeeeee! Zsh-zsh-zsh-WHIRRRRRRRRRR!*

"What a horrible noise!" gasped Rosso.

"Well, that will give *us* all a headache," groaned Gipsy. "But what effect will it have on the dino-droids?"

Suddenly the door burst open and the ankylosaur–droids strode inside.

*Ba-bump! Screeeeeeeeeeeee! Zsh-zsh!*

"They know we're up to something!" shouted Teggs.

Gipsy nodded. "Look out, Iggy,
they're coming after you!"

The pterosaur-droids flapped in. Their
red eyes span angrily.

"Try to boost the signal!" cried Arx.

Iggy quickly fiddled with his gadget.

Then suddenly the dino-droids
stopped their advance. Their red eyes
were turning a shocking shade of pink.
Smoke was curling from their metal
bodies.

"It's working!" yelled Gipsy over the
racket.

"Keep going, Iggy," Teggs urged him.

"More power!"

The noise got louder . . . *louder* . . . Then the dino-droids shook and shivered – and finally exploded! Nuts and bolts and springs and circuits blasted all around the room. When the smoke cleared, there was nothing left of them but a metal foot or a scorched wing here and there.

"It worked!" Gipsy cheered.

Rosso beamed. "Well done, Iggy!"

"Yes, well done, Iggy. We've got past the first hurdle," said Teggs. Iggy cut through his ropes with a bit of burnt metal, then they untied the others. "Now we must get after Attila and Draxie, right away."

Arx nodded. "But they will have taken the *Sauropod*!"

"They must have come here in some kind of spaceship," said Iggy. "It will be in the docking bay. Let's check it out!"

They raced through the deserted
corridors of the fake HQ, all the way
to the docking bay. But all they found
was an old, ramshackle shuttle.

"Oh," said Rosso. "Oh dear."

Teggs groaned. "How will we ever
catch them up in *that* old wreck?"

Gipsy rushed inside. "The radio is
broken," she called. "We can't even send
a warning to the real DSS HQ!"

"How long before the *Sauropod* gets
there?" asked Iggy.

"Depending on where we are in the Tyrannosaur Territories . . ." Rosso thought for a few seconds. "No longer than two days."

"The meeting will have started by then," Teggs realized. "The dino-droids will steam straight in and ruin everything. And there's nothing we can do!"

"There is, Captain," said Arx uneasily. "But it's dangerous. Very dangerous. *Extremely* dangerous. VERY *extremely* dangerous—"

"OK, Arx, I think we get the message," said Teggs. "What's your plan?"

"We take a short cut – through the space tunnel!"

The astrosaurs looked at him in disbelief.

"Travel through the space tunnel again?" boggled Iggy. "In *that* heap of old dung?"

Arx shrugged. "If we go through it from *this* side, we should come out back in the Vegetarian Sector, near Trimuda. And from there, we might just reach DSS HQ ahead of Attila."

"But the *Sauropod* was almost destroyed by the journey," Gipsy reminded him. "What chance do we stand in that rust-bucket?"

"A small chance," Arx admitted. "A very small chance. An *extremely* small chance. A—"

"Yes, yes, yes," Admiral Rosso interrupted. "But it's our *only* chance of stopping the dino-droids." He looked at each of the astrosaurs in turn. "This will be the most dangerous mission of our lives – and the most important."

"We're with you, sir," said Teggs. He gave his crew a crooked smile. "Let's do it!"

It didn't take long to get the little ship ready for blast-off. And it didn't take long to find the entrance to the space tunnel.

The crew waited in grim silence as Iggy steered them back towards the dark, sinister hole in space . . .

## Chapter Ten

# DESTINATION: DINO-DROIDS!

Soon, the rusty old shuttle was shaking and quaking like a jelly in an earthquake. On and on they went, picking up speed. The mouth of the space tunnel glowed with a strange, alien power as it drew them closer.

Suddenly a huge lump of rock shot past the ship's windscreen.

"Uh-oh!" shouted Teggs over the roar of the engines. "Looks like some stray meteors are being dragged through too!"

"That's all we need," groaned Gipsy. "If we're not squished into space junk by the space tunnel, a meteor will squash us instead!"

"Maybe not," said Arx. "In fact, a meteor might be just what we need. If we can only fly *inside* one, all that rock would help protect us as we go through the hole."

"Like a natural shield," Rosso agreed. "Good thinking, Arx!"

"First we have to find the right sort of meteor," Teggs warned them as the control room began to glow with heat.

"There's one!" bellowed Gipsy. She pointed to a huge jagged rock. It was filled with holes like a Swiss cheese.

"Great. Now we just have to fly inside it." Iggy took a deep breath. "Hold on tight, everyone!"

"We already are!" Gipsy cried as the ship lurched from side to side.

"Hold on even *tighter*, then!"

With incredible skill, Iggy steered the shaking ship into a deep split within the tumbling meteor. Then, with a horrible scraping sound like claws against a chalkboard, they came to a halt.

"We're jammed inside the split!" Iggy reported. "Right in the middle of the meteor."

"Good work, Iggy!" Teggs yelled. "All right, everyone, get ready and hope for the best. *We're passing back through the space tunnel!*"

Time slowed down. Every second seemed to last for hours. The ship stretched like old knicker elastic. Through the windows, they saw the rock glowing red-hot, then white. The controls inside started to melt . . .

Until finally – *WHOOOSH!* – the ship shot out the other side. The white-hot rock of their meteor shield crumbled away to space dust, sprinkling in their wake like a comet's tail.

"We did it!" Rosso shouted, and everyone cheered and whooped for joy.

"Good work, crew," Teggs agreed. "Arx, where are we now?"

"Flying away from Trimuda like a stone from a slingshot," the triceratops told him. "A lot of these controls aren't working . . . but I *think* we're on our way to DSS HQ!"

Teggs jumped in the air. "Brilliant!"

Gipsy nodded nervously. "But will we be in time?"

The journey seemed to last for ever. Gipsy kept trying the radio to see if she could send out a warning, but it was beyond repair. Only the engines were still working, just barely – spluttering like dragons with whooping cough. Luckily there was no shortage of fuel – Admiral Rosso hadn't "been" since he was kidnapped, and he soon made up for lost time.

Finally, Gipsy gave an excited shout. "DSS HQ! Look, it's straight ahead!"

"But the *Sauropod* has just arrived too," said Teggs grimly.

They could see their beautiful egg-shaped ship gliding gently into HQ's docking bay.

"We *must* stop Attila and his evil droids from leaving the ship," cried Rosso. "If they get into HQ, they will wreck the meeting!"

Iggy tapped the side of his snout knowingly. "Lucky we built that secret back door into the *Sauropod*, eh, Captain?"

Gipsy and Arx stared at Teggs in surprise. He shrugged and smiled. "I had it fitted in case we ever lost our keys."

Iggy zoomed right up to the egg-shaped ship and bumped against its bottom three times. A flap opened up to allow them into the dung-torpedo store.

"Brilliant!" cried Arx.

But as they landed they heard a loud *CLANG!*

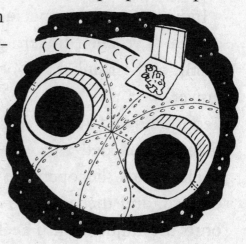

"The *Sauropod* has docked with HQ," said Arx breathlessly. "We might not be in time to stop them!"

"We have to try," said Teggs. "Gipsy, Admiral Rosso — head for the emergency exit and go straight to HQ. Explain to the VIDs what danger they're in." He nodded to Iggy and Arx. "As for you two — let's get to the flight deck. It's time to take on those dino-droids!"

Teggs led Arx and Iggy in a charge to the lifts, and bashed the button for the flight deck with the tip of his tail.

Iggy waggled his special jamming device. "I've been tinkering with this thing, and I think I've boosted the power."

"Good," said Teggs. "We need all the help we can get!"

The doors slid open the second they arrived, and the astrosaurs burst out onto the flight deck. The Teggs-droid

looked up from the control pit. The
Arx-droid span round in his chair. And
Draxie hopped from foot to foot,
spluttering in disbelief.

"You!" he cried. "How did *you* ever
get here?"

Teggs smiled. "Well if you will leave
space tunnels lying around . . . !"

The dimorphodon squawked in
alarm and surprise – they
thought they were
seeing double!

"It's all right,
boys," Teggs called.
"You've been taken
in by some diabolical
dino-droids. *We* are the real astrosaurs!"

"Don't listen to him," squeaked Draxie. "*They* are fakes!"

"Switch on your gadget, Iggy," cried Teggs. "We'll prove it!"

*Screeeeeeeeeeeeeee!* A dreadful din started up from the jamming device. The eyes of the droids turned red and started to spin round and round. The dimorphodon scattered, screeching in alarm.

Gas nozzles emerged from the Arx-droid's horns, just as Teggs had seen before. But the Teggs-droid had an altogether deadlier weapon to hand. Or rather, to *tail*. Its spiky tail split down the middle – to reveal a gigantic laser cannon!

"Look out!" bellowed Teggs, shoving Arx and Iggy to the ground as his

double opened fire.
A laser bolt sizzled
over their heads
and blew up the
wall behind them.

"I landed on the jamming device!"
wailed Iggy. "It's broken!"

"Fix it, fast," Teggs told him. "Arx, we
must buy him some time!"

"Your time is up, Captain Teggs,"
sneered Draxie. "Attila and the
Rosso-droid are already on their way
to the Pick-a-Planet meeting!"

Teggs frowned. "So where are your
droids of Gipsy and Iggy?"

"Right behind you, Captain," they
chorused from inside the lift. The dino-
droids' eyes were blazing red.

Without the jamming device, how
could they all be stopped?

## Chapter Eleven

# THE SHATTERING SHOWDOWN

Teggs whacked the Gipsy-droid on its oily hip, knocking it to the floor. Arx tried to charge at the Iggy-droid, but sparks of power burst from its claws, forcing him back.

The Gipsy-droid's head-crest opened up and fired a mini-missile at Teggs. He dodged aside – but fell straight into the path of the Arx-droid. The robot lowered its three-horned head, ready to gas him . . .

In the nick of time, some daring dimorphodon flapped by and shoved cotton wool down into the deadly nozzles! The dino-droid's eyes clouded over as the gas was forced back inside its body.

"Look out, Captain!" gasped the real Arx.

Teggs turned to find the Iggy-droid closing in, its electric claws outstretched. The Gipsy-droid was just behind it, aiming another missile.

And the Teggs-droid was coming to get him too, raising its terrifying tail cannon.

But at the last moment, just as his mirror image opened fire, Teggs dived into the control pit. The Iggy-droid was hit by the laser blast instead.

Its head exploded!

The robot's body went out of control, and its electric claws dug into the Gipsy-droid. Crackles of red energy surrounded them both, scrambling their circuits. With an electronic burp, six missiles shot from the fake Gipsy's forehead and the Arx-droid went up in smoke.

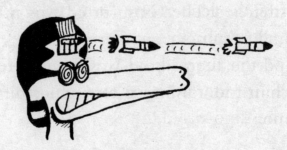

Only the Teggs-droid was left standing.

"Very clever, Captain," sneered Draxie. "But *your* double is the deadliest of all."

"It's certainly the best-looking!" joked Teggs as the dino-droid bore down on him.

But by now, Arx had recovered. He charged into the dino-droid's side, denting it badly. It staggered under the impact – straight into a tail-swipe from the real Teggs. Before the droid could react, Arx charged into it again, his mighty horns punching a hole in its metal hide. Then Sprite, the leader of the dimorphodon, flew right into the hole and started pecking at the dino-droid's insides with his

beak. The robot's movements grew
jerky and wild.

"Get out, Sprite!" Teggs yelled.

Sprite flapped out just in time. A few
moments later – *KA-BOOOM!* – the
dino-droid exploded into a billion bits.

"Whew!" said Teggs, wiping his brow.
"That was close!"

"Not fair!" wailed Draxie as the other
dimorphodon grabbed him with their
beaks and claws and held him prisoner.

"You may have got me – but you will never stop Attila!"

"We'll see about that," said Arx.

"I've fixed the jamming device," Iggy reported.

"Then what are we waiting for?" cried Teggs, bundling into the lift. "Let's move!"

Admiral Rosso and Gipsy charged through the broad, bright corridors of the real DSS HQ. Soon they ran into a group of ankylosaur guards, who stared at them in puzzlement.

"Hey, you!" Rosso peered down at the chief guard. "Have I passed by this way already?"

The chief guard gulped. "Er, yes, sir. About five minutes ago." He scratched his head. "In fact, sir, you're calling the Pick-a-Planet meeting to order right now!"

"Oh *no!*" bellowed Rosso. "Come on, Gipsy!"

They pushed past the guards and burst into the vast meeting room. Carnivores and plant-eaters alike jumped up in alarm and surprise.

"You!" gasped Attila, peeping out from behind the Rosso-droid.

"You're all being tricked!" thundered the admiral. "I am the *real* Rosso! That imposter is a dino-droid – a mere machine!"

"I am not!" retorted Rosso's dino-droid double. "Guards, arrest these intruders!"

Armed ankylosaurs swarmed into the room and grabbed hold of them.

"Let us go!" cried Gipsy. "You've got to believe us!"

"Pah!" Attila jumped on a table and waggled his silvery bum at her. "Why should we?"

"Because they're telling the truth!" came a familiar voice from the doorway.

It was Teggs!

He pushed his way into the room, Arx and Iggy just behind him.

"Arrest *these* intruders too!" rumbled the Rosso-droid. "They're nuts!"

"We'll see about that," said Iggy, switching on the jamming device. "This will *prove* that you're a dino-droid!"

*SCREEEEE!* The noise from the machine was even louder than before. *Ba-ba-bump!* Zsh-zsh-*WHIRRRRRR!* At once, the Rosso-droid's eyes began to burn flame-red and spin like crazy. It twitched and jerked like a puppet

with tangled strings. Then, with a
fizzling, sizzling sound, the robot started
to melt like an ice cream on a hot
day.

The meeting room grew even noisier
with gasps of fear and amazement
from the crowd.

"You see?" cried Arx. "It's a fake.
Iggy's machine is jamming its metal
mind!"

"What do you say to *that*, Attila?"
Teggs challenged.

"Well, thanks a lot for
spoiling my evil plans,"
snarled Attila as the
robot Rosso dissolved
into a big, bubbling
puddle. "But by
the stunning
stitching on my
silver shorts –
you'll never
get me!"

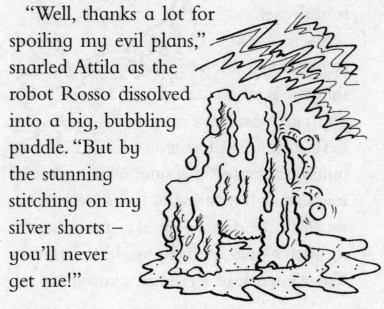

With that, the carnivore turned to run. But he couldn't. He struggled to get away, but it was no good. The sticky remains of his dino-droid had glued his feet to the ground!

Iggy turned off the jamming device with a quiet chuckle. "Looks like we're *stuck* with you, Attila!"

Everyone stared at the disco-dino in disbelief.

Then Rosso cleared his throat. "Right then, everybody. Let's start this meeting again, shall we?" he said, as if nothing much had happened. "Guards, clear away that horrible splodgy mess, lock up Attila and fetch me a clean chair. There's work to be done, planets to share out . . ." He smiled fondly at the *Sauropod* crew. "And many more adventures to be had."

"Very true, sir." Teggs nodded eagerly and licked his lips. "Once we've had a spot of breakfast, we'll be on our way!"

"Oh no, you won't," Rosso retorted. "You will stay for a special victory feast! I'm going to award each of you a very special medal – the Order of the Righteous Reptile."

Teggs gulped and stared around at his crew. "But . . . that's the highest honour an astrosaur can receive!"

"You've earned it," said the admiral firmly. Then he looked around at the startled VIDs staring on. "And for saving us all from a terrible space war, I think they've earned a round of applause too, don't you?"

The plant-eaters burst into wild claw-clapping. Slowly, even the carnivores joined in. Iggy took a bow,

and Gipsy curtseyed politely, while Teggs and Arx gave their stiffest dinosaur salutes. Attila glared at them as he was marched messily from the room.

"Well, that was a medal-winning adventure, all right," Teggs declared as the applause went on and on. "And after a fabulous feast and forty winks, this righteous reptile will be ready for another one . . . *double* quick!"

**THE END**

# TALKING DINOSAUR!

STEGOSAURUS –
*STEG-oh-SORE-us*

BAROSAURUS –
*bar-oh-SORE-us*

HADROSAUR –
*HAD-roh-sore*

DIMORPHODON –
*die-MORF-oh-don*

IGUANODON –
*ig-WA-noh-don*

TRICERATOPS –
*try-SERRA-tops*

ANKYLOSAURUS –
*an-KI-loh-SORE-us*

DRACOPELTA –
*dray-ko-PEL-ta*

TYRANNOSAUR –
*tie-RAN-oh-SORE*

DASPLETOSAURUS –
*dass–PLEE-tuh-SAWR-us*

PTEROSAUR –
*TEH-roh-sore*

THEROPOD –
*THER-uh-pod*

# ASTROSAURS

## BOOK EIGHT

# THE TERROR-BIRD TRAP

Read the first chapter here!

## Chapter One

## THE SHORE OF SECRETS

Captain Teggs stared out of the shuttle window at the picture-perfect view. Three suns lit the bright blue sky. The sea sparkled like it was full of emeralds. Tiny tropical islands lay dotted all around.

"So this is the planet Atlantos," he said, frowning.

"It looks far too *nice* for a rough, tough mission. It's the sort of place you go to have a . . . a—" He pulled a face, as if the words tasted bad. "A *holiday*!"

Gipsy playfully threw a beach ball at his head. "A little holiday wouldn't hurt you, Captain."

"Gipsy's right," said Iggy, his claws gripping the shuttle's joystick as he steered. "You haven't had a day off since you took charge of the *Sauropod*!"

"Who needs a day off?" said Teggs. "Righting wrongs and fighting villains isn't hard work – it's fun!" He batted the beach ball over to Arx. "What do you think, Arx?"

Arx balanced the ball on the biggest of his three grey horns. "It's just a

feeling, Captain, but I think this mission may be one of our most dangerous yet."

Teggs looked at Arx thoughtfully. The triceratops's instincts were strong, and if he smelled trouble ahead, he was probably right.

*Hooray!*

Iggy pointed to an island that was bigger than all the others. "There's our destination," he said. "Kleen Island."

"Well, we've got here at top speed in the shuttle, just as we were told," said Teggs. "Now all we need to know is *why*. I wish Admiral Rosso would hurry up and tell us."

"I'm sure he'll be in touch soon," said Gipsy. She picked up a bucket and spade. "And while we're waiting – we can *play*!"

Iggy landed the shuttle on a beautiful

beach, and the astrosaurs went outside into the triple-sunshine. The place was deserted. While Arx and Iggy explored over by some steep white cliffs, Gipsy went paddling at the sea's edge. Teggs chased after her, splashing water over her with his big spiky tail. As he did so, he heard something crack beneath his feet.

"Hey, this isn't sand I'm standing

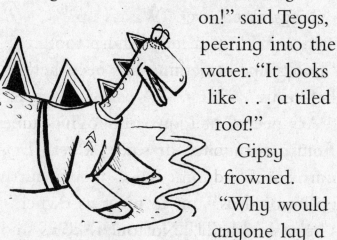

on!" said Teggs, peering into the water. "It looks like . . . a tiled roof!"

Gipsy frowned.

"Why would anyone lay a roof under water?"

"I don't know," said Teggs. He paddled over to the edge of the roof. Then he dipped his head beneath the waves for a few seconds and looked around. "A whole *street* has been built under here!" he spluttered. "Think of the problems the owners must have with damp!"

"Maybe that's why there's no one about," said Gipsy, glancing round nervously.

"Hey, Captain!" called Iggy, breaking the silence.

Teggs raced over. "What's up?"

Iggy held up a large, sharp tooth. "Looks like something has been here before us."

Arx peered at Iggy's find. "This came from a carnivore," he said. "A very *large* carnivore."

"I wouldn't want to meet its owner." Gipsy shuddered. "Not unless *all* its teeth have fallen out!"

"If there are carnivores about, maybe that explains why no one is here," said Teggs. "We'd better get back to the shuttle and change into combat gear."

Suddenly, the ground began to tremble beneath them. Then it lurched. The astrosaurs staggered sideways.

"What was *that*?" asked Iggy, as the tremors died away. "An earthquake?"

"I don't think so." Teggs frowned, shifting his weight between his four enormous feet. "The whole island feels like it's tipped to one side!"

Read the rest of
**THE TERROR-BIRD TRAP**
to find out what terrors await the
team on Atlantos!

Fantastic **Astrosaurs** collector cards –
your mission is to collect them all!
Cards are available in every **Astrosaurs**
book and for more free cards log onto
www.**astrosaurs**.co.uk